SNUG AND SERENA
COUNT TWELVE

SNUG AND SERENA COUNT TWELVE

BY

ALISON UTTLEY

ILLUSTRATED BY

KATHERINE WIGGLESWORTH

 THE **BOBBS-MERRILL** COMPANY, INC.
A SUBSIDIARY OF HOWARD W. SAMS & CO., INC.
Publishers • INDIANAPOLIS • NEW YORK

Library of Congress Catalog Card No.: 62-19331
Copyright © 1959, 1962 by Alison Uttley and
Katherine Wigglesworth
All rights reserved
Printed in the United States of America
First Edition

SNUG AND SERENA
COUNT TWELVE

"Snug and Serena ought to go to
school," said Mrs. Mouse one day.
The two little mice put down their
spoons and listened. Their eyes
shone, their tails twitched, and they
licked their lips with excitement.

"School? What for?" asked Mr.
Mouse.

"To learn things," said Mrs. Mouse.

"What things?" demanded Mr.
Mouse. "They can learn enough

at home without going to school. They can fetch and carry, and run errands. They can sweep the floor, and dust the chairs, and make straw mats as well as anybody. They can carve chestnuts into baskets, and polish hazelnuts and collect cherry stones."

Snug and Serena opened wide their eyes as Mr. Mouse told of their cleverness. He had never mentioned it before.

"That is not enough," said Mrs. Mouse, firmly.

8

"What else?" asked Mr. Mouse, impatiently. "They can find herbs and bring them home to make dandelion soda and herb tea, and root beer, and wild mustard plaster."

"Go on with your breakfasts," said Mrs. Mouse to Snug and Serena, and they went on.

"They ought to know how to count," said Mrs. Mouse.

"I can teach them to count," said Mr. Mouse, gruffly. He went to the dresser and took down the blue mugs.

"One mug for John Barleycorn," said he, thumping a mug on the table.

"One for Jonathan Furze, and one for Samuel."

He went on banging the table with a mug as he spoke.

"That's three mugs."

"That's only counting up to three," objected Mrs. Mouse. "There's more than three in the world."

Mr. Mouse ran to the shelf where the blue mugs were ranged in a row.

"One mug for Mr. Toad, and one for you, my dear. That's five mugs,"

11

said he, triumphantly, as he banged
down two more mugs.

Snug and Serena giggled, but Mr.
Mouse frowned at them.

"There are more mugs left,

12

William," said Mrs. Mouse, quietly.
"Go on with your counting."

Mr. Mouse stamped across the
floor and took two more mugs.

"A mug for Snug and one for
Serena to drink new milk in," said
he. "That's two mugs."

"No, it's seven," said Snug. "Mr.
Toad told me."

"No mouse has ever been known
to count more than five," said Mr.
Mouse. "After five we begin again.
We've had five, and now we begin
again. A toad may count more but
mice don't."

"Let us go to school, please," cried
Serena. "We want to count lots
and lots."

"We will ask Mr. Toad for advice,"
said Mrs. Mouse. "He will know
about such things."

All that day Snug and Serena
scampered about counting things.
When they got up to five they
hesitated and when they got to seven
they stopped.

14

"Mr. Toad will help us," they said.

Next day Mr. Toad came and
Serena ran to meet him.

"Well, little Serena, you are in a
hurry," said Mr. Toad, pleasantly,
and he put his thumbs in his
waistcoat and looked at the eager
little mouse. Snug came hurrying
after her.

"Please, Mr. Toad, I want to go to
school," said Serena, "and so does

15

Snug. Both of us. One, two of us."

"I'll give you some lessons," said
Mr. Toad, puffing out his chest.

"We want to do counting," said
Serena.

"Counting? Why?" asked the fat
old toad. "I've already taught you to
count up to seven, which is the
magic number. Seven stars in the
Great Bear up in the sky. Seven
nuts in a hazel bunch. Seven cows

16

in our field. Seven pigs in the pigsty. Seven mugs on your dresser."

1 2 3 4 5 6 7.

"We want to know how many crows are flying and how many bees in a swarm," said Serena.

"And how many blackbirds in the

17

hedges, and how many worms in
the ground," added Snug.

"And how many fish in the river,"
said Serena, "and how many frogs
in the marsh, and how many toads
. . . toads . . . toads . . ."

"There is only one toad and that's
me," said Mr. Toad. "The others
don't count.

18

"And there's only one Policeman
Owl in the wood but there's a
Hunting Owl in the lane. He doesn't
count.

"Luckily only one fierce weasel lives
in that house in the rocks."

He hesitated and looked down at
the two small mice.

"I know a clever animal who will
teach you to count," said he, kindly.
"It is true I only count up to seven
but this animal knows more. She's
a bit strange in her ways, a foreigner,
but she can count. I'll talk it over

20

with your mother. I am not sure, indeed I am not sure, but perhaps . . . perhaps . . ."

He went home with the two little mice.

Mr. Mouse was polishing the blue mugs and saying, "One, two, three, four, five. One, two. That makes sense, that does. Where does seven come in?"

Mrs. Mouse was calming him
down.

"Oh, Mr. Toad," she cried, as Mr.
Toad, with Snug and Serena hanging
on to his coat tails, entered.

"Yes, I know," said Mr. Toad.
"It's this schooling, isn't it?"

"Yes, will you give us some
advice?" asked Mr. Mouse. "Snug
says you have taught him to count

22

seven. He says there are seven mugs
on my sideboard."

"Mr. Mouse, William," began Mr.
Toad. "I think you ought to let your
children go to school and learn to
count. I know of a teacher, a clever
animal, but . . . but . . . she's
different from us."

"In what way?" asked Mrs.
Mouse, anxiously.

23

"She's a refugee. She's **away from** home. She's a town mouse living in the country," said Mr. Toad.

"Poor thing," said Mrs. Mouse. "A refugee."

"She pines for her own life, but she dare not return. She came to live here a week ago. She is very clever. She could teach our little mice to count," said Mr. Toad.

He talked it over privately with Mr. and Mrs. Mouse, and they agreed to send Snug and Serena to the town mouse's cottage.

"She is very sharp and quick-tempered, but she has a lot of knowledge through living in the

24

same house as human beings," said Mr. Toad.

"In the same house as those giants?" cried Mr. Mouse.

"Yes, it's her house, but she allows them to live there. However, somebody else—a cat—came there and she found she couldn't share her house with the—er—er—somebody else," said Mr. Toad. "So she packed

25

her bag and came to the lane, to take an empty cottage under the honeysuckle."

Mr. and Mrs. Mouse nodded.

"You can trust her. She has a birch rod for discipline, and a corner for naughty mice, and she can count," said Mr. Toad.

"Well, I agree to that," said Mr. Mouse. "Some discipline will do

26

Snug and Serena good. As for counting, well, let them count."

So Snug and Serena prepared for school. They went to the woods to find pencils and slates. The pencils were sharp pointed little sticks with which they could write in the sandy ground. The slates were thin layers of shale from a cutting in the old quarry. Snug and Serena found half a dozen little square slabs of stone, thin as wafers, all ready for use. There were many more stored under the grassy edge of the sandstone.

"We can write on these with some bits of hard stone," said Snug, and they picked up some splinters of

27

stone and scribbled on the stone
slates.

Mrs. Mouse knew where there was
a pile of cherry stones bleached by

the sun, smooth as ivory. They had been left by the field mice when they ate the fallen wild cherries in the woods.

"These are for counting," said she, and Snug and Serena filled two school bags with them.

There was a bat's-wing purse to hold their school money, and a woven grass bag to hold their slates and pencils. The school money was mice money, which is the seeds of buttercups and wild mustard and other plants.

Snug and Serena were washed
and scrubbed. Snug had a new
handkerchief and Serena a new
pinafore, so they looked neat and
pretty as they set off to school with
Mrs. Mouse and Mr. Toad to take
them there on the first day.

They all went down the lane,
through a honeysuckle archway to a
small cottage hidden in the bank
among ferns and mosses.

30

Mrs. Town Mouse, who felt the drafts of the country, had brought in sheep's wool to make carpets and curtains, and pieces of wood for floors, and pieces of wastepaper for bedding.

Mr. Toad rapped at the door and Mrs. Mouse sniffed a little.

31

"Stuffy," said she. "Not enough fresh air for a country mouse."

Mrs. Town Mouse answered the door. She was delighted to see company, and she invited them all inside.

"I have brought my children to be your pupils," said Mrs. Mouse, softly. "Mr. Toad said you would teach them to count."

"Certainly," said Mrs. Town Mouse, looking at Snug and Serena with her sharp little eyes. "I am a great counter. I shall be glad to teach your pretty children."

"Then I will leave them in your charge, thank you. Send them home in good time for dinner, Mrs. Town Mouse. They have their school money in their purses," said Mrs. Mouse.

Mrs. Mouse and Mr. Toad went away and Snug and Serena were left. Snug darted round the room

looking at everything and Serena
began to dance.

"Stop!" cried Mrs. Town Mouse.
"Sit still! I can't teach you if you
dance about like this. You must
learn to be quiet."

She was so stern the two mice sat
silently on the low seats.

They had to keep so still they
thought they would be changed into
stone.

"When a fierce animal looks at
you, he won't see you if you keep
still," said Mrs. Town Mouse,
severely. "You must first learn to
be still."

"A hawk once carried me off," said

34

Snug, jumping up. "I got home again, and I left my jacket behind on the church steeple."

"Silence!" cried Mrs. Town Mouse. "It is possible to escape from a hawk, but you could not get away from a cat."

"Please, can we do counting?"

piped Serena. "I don't want to hear about cats."

Mrs. Town Mouse frowned. "A cat is a very fierce animal. It eats the mice in one gulp. It is an ogre, a dragon, and its eyes are like green fires. Its teeth are like white swords, and its tongue like a red flame."

"I should like to meet a cat," said Snug. "I'm not afraid. Now let's go on to counting."

"You boastful mouse," said Mrs. Town Mouse, crossly.

She trotted away and fetched her bead frame for counting. Serena and Snug emptied their cherry stones from their bags. The lesson began.

The mice made little piles of white cherry stones, and Mrs. Town Mouse counted with them. She taught them a song as they darted here and there carrying the little stones.

"One, two, three, four,
Mouses at their mother's door.

Five, six, seven, eight,
Cherry stones are on a plate.

37

Nine, ten, eleven, twelve,
Mouses dig and mouses delve.

Twelve's a dozen, please remember,
All the months till cold
December.

"That's enough for today," said
Mrs. Town Mouse. "You have learned
a dozen, and that is a big number."

"How many stars in the sky?"
asked Snug, collecting his cherry

38

stones and putting them back in his bag.

"Lots of dozens. Lots of twelves," said Mrs. Town Mouse.

"How many fishes in the river?" asked Serena.

"You must go there and find out," said Mrs. Town Mouse, impatiently.

"The three old mice went fishing with my Father and caught some big ones," said Snug.

"Don't talk about fish," shuddered Mrs. Town Mouse. "We had plenty of fish in our house, but it was food for the cat. Don't mention it."

"Can we talk about stars?" asked Serena. "Did your cat eat stars?"

"She might," said Mrs. Town
Mouse. "She prowled at night when
the stars came out and sometimes
she and her friends gave a concert
of horrible music on the roof. She
sang so loudly we shivered in our
home under the floor."

40

"Come again tomorrow," said Mrs. Town Mouse, as they paid their mouse pennies. "I will teach you to count more numbers."

"I like counting," said Snug. "I'm glad there are more numbers to learn."

"Goodbye, Mrs. Town Mouse," said Serena. "Have we been good?"

"Yes, fairly good," said Mrs. Town Mouse, and she yawned and shut her eyes. The two little mice tripped away.

41

They sang their counting song, but somehow they got it all wrong.

"One, two, three, four,
Pussy at the mouse's door.

Five, six, seven, eight,
Eating mouses off a plate.

Nine, ten, eleven, twelve,
Pussy smiles and licks herself.

Mouses gone and so are we,
We are going home to tea."

They went along the lane, chattering about numbers and they counted the things they saw. One robin sang its gay song, and two

42

COUNT TWELVE

cuckoos shouted "Cuckoo" in the wood.

43

Three crows flew across the sky,

and four snails crept among the leaves.

Five calves looked over a wall,

and six pigeons sat in a high fir tree.

Seven little rabbits danced in the field,

and eight baby ducklings swam in
the stream.

Nine frogs hopped in the marsh,

and ten butterflies flitted overhead.

Eleven ants searched on the ground

and twelve bees were making honey.

They dawdled among the company
of birds and insects, the flowers and
small animals, counting and singing
a new song, much easier than Mrs.
Town Mouse's.

"One robin in a tree,
Two cuckoos shout to me.

Three crows up in the sky,
Four snails come crawling by.

Five calves look over a wall,
Six pigeons croon and call.

Seven rabbits on the green,
Eight ducklings swim the stream.

Nine frogs in marshy bed,
Ten butterflies overhead.

Eleven ants look for money,
Twelve bees are after honey."

They got home at last. It was
late and Mrs. Mouse was at the door
looking for them.

"Here you come. Mrs. Town Mouse
kept you a long time," said Mrs.
Mouse. "Have you had any dinner?"

50

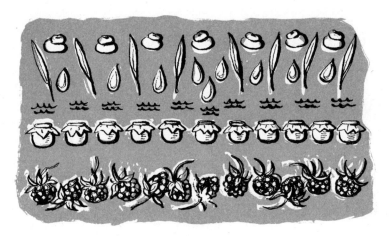

"Oh, yes. We had twelve wild strawberries, and eleven pots of honey, and ten sips of water and nine drops of honeydew, and eight blades of grass and seven loaves of bee-bread," began Snug in a hurry.

"We can count, Mother, up to twelve," said Serena, excitedly. "We've been counting all the way

51

home. Everything is part of counting."

"Well, come in and have your tea, and count the slices of bread and butter," laughed Mrs. Mouse. "Mr. Toad has been waiting to see you."

The old toad rose to his feet as they entered.

"My little Serena! My little Snug!" said he. "I have been worried about you. Was the town mouse easy with you? Did she use the birch rod?"

"Oh, no, Mr. Toad. She was kind and she taught us lots of counting," said Serena.

"One Mr. Toad. Two little brown mice. Three old mice," began Snug

52

as Samuel and Timothy and John Barleycorn came in to hear the news.

"Four cups on the table, five chairs in the kitchen, six candles in the cupboard, seven mugs on the shelf," said Serena, hurriedly.

"Stop! Don't count any more. I feel dizzy," said Mr. Mouse, as he brought a bottle of sweet primrose soda from the cellar for the three old mice to sip.

They all sat round the table, eight of them, and Mrs. Mouse gave them wild strawberry jam and little cheese cakes, and rolls of wheat bread with dandelion salad.

53

Afterwards Snug and Serena sang the song Mrs. Town Mouse had taught them, but it was still all wrong.

"One, two, three, four,
Weasels tapping at my door.

Five, six, seven, eight,
Cats and owls are never late.

Nine, ten, eleven, twelve,
Mouses dig and Mouses delve."

"We know that song," said the old mice. "Listen to us." They

54

croaked and wheezed, and sang in shrill high trebles:

"One, two, three, four,
Harvest mice upon the floor.

Five, six, seven, eight,
Eating cheese upon a plate.

Nine, ten, eleven, twelve,
If you want any more you must
    sing it yourselves."

"How many stars in the sky, Snug?" asked Mr. Toad slyly when the two little mice were ready for bed.

"Dozens and dozens," said Snug.

"Mrs. Town Mouse is going to count them for us," said Serena.

"Then you'll want lots of cherry stones," said Mr. Toad.

But Mrs. Town Mouse did not count them, nor did Snug and Serena have any more lessons from her.

"Too-whit. Too-whoo," cried the owl that night, and he flew down the

lane with his white wings spread, as
he hunted for a nice fat mouse.

Mrs. Town Mouse shivered and
pulled the curtains close and locked
the door.

"Too-whit. Too-whoo," hooted the
owl. "I've heard there's a fat town
mouse down here."

Mrs. Mouse began to pack her
clothes and her bits of things.

"Sniff! Sniff!" went the weasel. "There's a town mouse all stout and plump. I must catch her tomorrow."

The weasel ruffled the leaves in the hedge bottom, and Mrs. Mouse crouched in the depths of her hole.

At dawn she ventured out. She carried her belongings in a bag and ran as fast as she could back to the town house.

"A cat in the kitchen is better than an owl in the lane and a weasel at your door," said she, as she

slipped through a hole in the wall. "There's better food at home. I'm going back."

So that is why Snug and Serena never counted the stars in the sky or the fish in the river or the daisies in the fields.

59

"You know quite enough for two little field mice," said Mr. Toad. "I'll teach you the names of the stars."

He began at the Great Bear and he told them about the Dog Star, and the Swan, the Heavenly Twins and Pegasus the Horse. The little mice with their bright eyes could see these great pictures in the starry sky and they did not trouble to count the stars.